THE CROSSOVER:

A BRIDGE FROM
THE COURT TO LIFE

BY: TRAVIS GARRISON

Lightning Fast Book Publishing, LLC

P.O. Box 441328

Fort Washington, MD 20744

www.lfbookpublishing.com

The author of this book gives applicable life lessons from basketball instruction. The literary offering provided is derived from the life experiences of the author. The intent is to aid the reader in developing athletically, and in character. In the event that you use or enact any of the material in this book, the author and publisher assume no responsibility for your actions.

This is a work of non-fiction.

The publisher, Lightning Fast Book Publishing, assumes no responsibility for any content presented in this book.

Table of Contents

Introduction

Having been a former basketball player, I've learned many different skills and techniques on the court. Mastering these skills and techniques led to a successful career in high school, college, and professionally. However, there were many times when I wanted to quit or give up. When I wanted to, I would always remember my coach telling me, *"It's not over until the last buzzer!"* There is no truer statement than this.

Throughout my career, I've discovered that the same skills and fundamentals I learned on the court could also help me off the court. This is the approach I have been using towards all obstacles in my life. The hundreds of hours of practice didn't just stay on the court, they transferred into my life. This not only made me a more rounded player, but also a better human being.

In reality, you are the only one who controls your life, through the actions that you take and through what comes out of your mouth. Therefore, as you read this book, remember that you can make personal changes whenever you want. Moreover, there is a life outside of the court, and as you journey through this book, take time to reflect, make connections to your own personal situations, and write your thoughts as you read along.

My goal for this book is to teach you that the same tools you learn to use for basketball can be used in your life off the court. Ultimately, I don't just want you to be a great and skilled basketball player. I want you to be a great student and a great kid on and off the court.

Dribbling

The Foundation

To be a good dribbler, you need a good, strong base to help you control the basketball. This strong base is also known as a high squat. When you are in a high squat, you are able to have more control of your legs, and while dribbling, you can move faster up and down the court, switch hands, and go between the legs. Having this type of strong foundation is critical to being successful in dribbling and basketball in general. On the other hand, if you are standing straight and tall, you have less control, and you are not able to go in between the legs while dribbling. As important as it is to have control of the ball while dribbling, it is even more essential to have control in other parts of your life. These include having control over your health, what you eat, and the surroundings you put yourself in.

Being a strong example of someone who is in control goes beyond the court. In the same way that your coach focuses intently on how you are dribbling, it is crucial that you are equally focused on how you are in control of everything else. If you focus on controlling all aspects of your life, you will not only become successful across the board, but you will become influential in the lives of other people and other players. This will only positively support your quest of being a great basketball player. This type of role model isn't always present, but there are players who exhibit control on and off the court. Therefore, always remember that having control over a basketball as well as things like finances, friendships, and life in general is what makes a basketball player even stronger.

How will you build a strong foundation?

_____

_____

_____

_____

_____

_____

_____

_____

_____

_____

The Purpose

The purpose of dribbling is to get the basketball from one end of the court to the other. While playing in a game, you want to run the offense in order to score. Understanding the purpose of dribbling in basketball can be linked to having a purpose in other areas of your life and understanding what it takes to meet that purpose. When dribbling, the purpose is to move the ball. In life, what is your purpose?

To play basketball in any academic setting, you have to be a serious student. However, being a student while also being an active athlete on a team involves real work. Just like dribbling requires a good high squat, being a serious student has requirements.

Going to class is a top requirement. However, just being there isn't the same as really participating. You have to dribble the ball while in the game, which is how you participate. In the same way, earning good grades while in class by completing homework is part of attending class and participating. If your coach asks you to go home, practice, and read and watch plays, this is homework for basketball. I doubt you'd tell the coach that you are too busy or get home too late to do the homework they are requesting to be completed. If you didn't understand the purpose of dribbling, you'd probably ask the necessary questions to gain a better understanding. Therefore, the habit of completing the work needed to be a serious student transfers equally to becoming a stronger basketball player. Whoever is dribbling the ball controls what is going on in the game. A studious student has better control over his or her ability to stay active on a basketball team, which should be one of the most important goals as a player.

Dribbling Failures

Learning how to dribble takes time. It is not something that you will have complete control over after a few minutes. There are many successful basketball players who dribbled poorly when they started. However, they didn't pass the ball to someone else and walk off the basketball court. They decided to continue practicing the skill from morning until night. They knew that having control of the ball was too important of a technique to not put time and effort into developing. In life, there are many failures and setbacks that make us lose our control and can lead us to give up. Instead of passing to someone else something that you have failed to do, keep on trying to gain control. This can be accomplished in a number of ways.

First, you can refocus to gain back control. You have to have tunnel vision when it comes to gaining control. Just like dribbling, you have to reset yourself if you are not in control of the ball. This could mean that you have to reset how you are squatting to get better control. If you are struggling with an assignment for school, you can reset yourself by asking the teacher for clarification. You can also ask your teacher to model how to do it, just like your coach would with dribbling.

You may also have to take a step back and think of a new plan. You may have to move laterally instead of horizontally due to a defender or obstacle in your way. You can't always just run up and down the court to reach your goal of taking and making a shot. So, if you've failed an assignment, what new plan can you create to help you earn a better grade? If you have had an argument with a friend and now you two are not talking, what new plan can you make to get the friendship back?

What moves can be taken to regain control?

_____

_____

_____

_____

_____

_____

_____

_____

_____

You can also work on strengthening weak spots by practicing harder. If you practice dribbling for hours, by the end you will be in better control than you were when you started. If you practice how to solve math problems, you will be in better control of your math skills than you were at the starting point. This developed idea to gain control can work in any other aspect of your life, especially if you want to be successful.

Life has many failures, and how you respond to them is important. Staying in control and having options for moving forward will only strengthen you mentally and physically. You will be a better controlled basketball player by not giving up and passing the ball off to someone you think is stronger or more skilled than you when you fail. An advanced dribbler will stick to the technique by staying low and keeping his or her fingers spread and relaxed. They will also learn how to move the ball through their legs and behind their back. They will also be able to change the pace of the ball handling while dribbling. Just like you want to become an advanced basketball player who is control, you also want to be a serious student athlete who is in control of their schoolwork and their emotions.

How will you overcome in life?

_____

_____

_____

_____

_____

_____

_____

_____

_____

_____

Checking Emotions

While dribbling, you have to stay calm and in control. Always remember your training and trust in it. If you are about to panic while dribbling, remind yourself that you are built to do it. If you begin to lose your emotions while taking a test, talking with your parents, or while involved in an altercation, you will lose control of your words, body, and feelings. The moment you stray away from what you have been trained to do in any given situation, you will fail. Your emotions can take control and the next thing you know, you have done something that you 100% wished you hadn't. Therefore, how do you keep your emotions under control?

One way to keep your emotions under control is to focus on breathing. Once you stop breathing, your body starts to tense up because it lacks oxygen. Another way to keep your emotions under control is to follow the techniques and fundamentals you have already learned. In basketball, if you forget what you have practiced, the outcomes on the court won't be in your favor. In life, we should remember what we were taught and keep it close to us. When we are in situations that aren't good for us, we have to stay in control to get out of those situations. Another way to keep your emotions in check is to take a break. Removing yourself from a situation that is not supporting your growth or overall well-being is the best thing you can do. This will help you keep your emotions in check because you are able to avoid negative situations altogether. Ultimately, you want to stay in control, and you need to do whatever is necessary to keep yourself in control.

How will you check your emotions?

_____

_____

_____

_____

_____

_____

_____

_____

Shooting

The Fundamentals

When you take a shot, you need to be confident in your movements. If you are at the rim, then you want to use your legs to get higher on the jump. Moreover, you want to make sure that your shot has a strong arc by making an arc with your hand. Your arm should be vertical and in line with the basket while your hand is arced over in the direction of the hoop. This arc has to be strong. You want your finger in the rim, so imagine putting your finger inside of the rim. By doing this, you know that you are high and strong enough. Regardless of where you are shooting from, you want to make sure that you're stable, in control, and ready to take the shot, regardless of the outcome.

A great example of an advanced shooter is Steph Curry. He is as successful as he is because of his hard work and dedication to the game. Since he is a short and slim guard, he is able to use his quickness and ball handling skills to get whatever kind of shot he wants. That is all a result of the time he spent in the gym working on his ball handling skills, as well as the hundreds of shots he made during practice. His hard work and dedication to the game resulted in his unanimous MVP honors and 4 NBA Championships. He is also considered one of the best shooters the NBA has ever had. The best part is that he is still young and has a lot more he can accomplish.

How will you build a strong foundation?

_____

_____

_____

_____

_____

_____

_____

_____

_____

The Purpose

The purpose of a shot is to score points for your team So that, ultimately, you help your team to win the game. This can only be done by taking shots and not stopping until the clock has run out. In life, we must take shots to get to the next level. We can't remain stationary and believe that something great will happen.

We take a shot every time we wake up and get out of bed. This shot represents a step in our daily morning routines. When we go to school, we take a shot every time we attend class. The goal is to make the shot, so when you are at school, you make the grades by showing up, studying, and having confidence in yourself. This isn't done by taking and passing one test. This is done over a period of time, just like in the game of basketball. Even if you miss a basket, you can get the ball back and take another shot. Equally, if you fail a test, quiz, or an assignment, take another shot at the next opportunity. Just because something happened to you in the past, that doesn't mean it will happen to you again. And even if it does happen again, keep taking shots and never give up!

Maybe you have been thinking about colleges, but you're worried about the expense. Are you still going to take a shot to see if you can get accepted and find scholarships or other ways to fund your education? If you never try to see what you can do, you will never move from the place you are in. Don't let the actual shot scare you. Focus more on taking the shot then the shot itself. You never know. You may apply and get accepted into your dream college! That college may offer you money to help pay your tuition or you might be able to find a job that will pay for it. Regardless, you won't know if you don't take a shot!

Shot Failures

When you miss a shot, it may be due to a number of things. If you don't follow through, then you may not make the shot. Let's say that your arm is aligned with the basket, but you don't execute a good wrist flick. Without the tight wrist flick, your arc isn't stabilized, which could cause you to miss the shot. If you have the arc but aren't able to maintain and hold it, then you may miss the basket. You also have to make sure that you know the angle and jump high enough to make the shot. If you don't, you may end up overextending your legs, so you have to be sure to jump the right height to get the reach you need. Never forget that it is all about angles and your legs!

Sometimes, you've done everything correctly and the ball still doesn't go in. Hey, it happens all the time. You could have practiced shooting for over 1,000 hours, but that doesn't mean you will make all your shots. Sometimes the ball just doesn't want to go in. Once, shooting guard Ray Allen missed 14 shots in one game. When reporters approached him the next day and asked why he had such a bad shooting night, he responded to them by saying "I didn't have a bad shooting night, the ball just doesn't go in". This is absolutely true! Sometimes the actual shot may be out of your hands, literally.

How will you overcome in life?

_____

_____

_____

_____

_____

_____

_____

_____

Checking Emotions

To take a shot, you need confidence. This confidence comes from a lot of practice. No one gets on the basketball court and makes every shot every time they shoot, especially someone who is brand new to the game. Do you think Steph Curry is the same player today as he was when he first began? He has dedicated his entire life to basketball and has played just as long. If there is a lack of practice, you will miss shots due to a lack of technique. At this point, do you get mad and give up? Do you yell at everyone or everything in your path? I surely hope not, especially if you didn't practice. And, even if you did spend countless hours studying or practicing, just remember that nothing is 100% all the time. You need to bounce back quickly if you miss a shot so that you can keep your momentum going.

In life, when we take shots, we don't know if we are going to make them all. However, if you have prepared adequately, then you will keep your confidence when you miss the shots you take. If you studied a lot and felt like you knew everything for an upcoming test, but you get the graded test back and realize that you answered questions wrong, what do you do? Do you lose all of your confidence and quit, or do you figure out a new plan so you will be successful the next time? A shooter won't be successful unless they have someone there to give them critiques, support, and encouragement. If you can't figure it out yourself, ask for help from someone else. But, let's say that you did earn the grade you wanted on the test. That wasn't done out of luck! It was done because you took the time to prepare yourself, just like a shooter takes the time to work on shooting before the big game.

Furthermore, you may want to take a shot and open a business, try a new haircut, cook a nice dinner for someone, or just go after your dreams. However, sometimes people might not believe in you and your dreams or may not feel the same way you feel about them. They may try to discourage you, tell you to never go after them, or complain to you about how they didn't reach their goals. Regardless of whatever negative things they say to you, don't allow them to block you from taking a shot! At the end of the day, you have to live your life. Make sure that you are doing whatever you want that makes you happy and supports a progressive future.

On the other end, one bad shot can cost you your life. If you spend your time trying to figure out how to cheat on an assignment, that may lead to you getting a failing grade. If you focus on how to take from others, your shots may be met with disappointment, anger, and resentment. If you hang out with the wrong people and take a shot by deciding to commit a crime with them, you, not them, may end up in jail, and the "friends" you thought you had will scatter faster than a crowd caught in the rain. Just remember, whatever you are focusing on, you will attempt to work towards. Therefore, you have to remind and ask yourself if what you are doing will have a good or bad outcome if you take a shot. You don't want to waste time taking shots at something that isn't good for you or your well-being. Make sure that you are preparing for something that is worthy of your shots.

How will you check your emotions?

_____

_____

_____

_____

_____

_____

_____

_____

Pivot

The Fundamentals

A pivot occurs when a player plants one foot while moving the other foot around. The pivot foot (planted foot) can't be lifted off the floor, nor can the position of the pivot foot change once it has been established. However, the player can rotate around the pivoted foot. In life, we will have to navigate around many things that come against us. When this happens, we must stay planted in our foundation and not waver from it. For example, even though your friends may be talking negatively about another friend, you must stay firm in your respect for others and not join the negative crowd.

Just like a pivot foot is planted on the ground unable to move, your foundation should be rooted in truth, honesty, and awareness. This will help prevent you from being forced into a direction that you don't want to go in. Even though you will encounter defenders, you can't allow them to distract you from your foundation and stance. Just like defenders on the court, there are many distractions in life. These distractions can be a girl or boy you like, or expensive shoes you may not be able to afford. Regardless of what the distractions are, they will always be present. Therefore, it is very important to be aware of the distractions, but not allow them to control your next move.

How will you build a strong foundation?

_____

_____

_____

_____

_____

_____

_____

_____

_____

_____

The Purpose

The purpose of pivoting is to avoid defensive players. You want to avoid a defensive player because they may be trying to steal the ball from you, attempting to block your shot, or attempting to cause a foul. This same idea of avoidance can be used off the court as well. When you want to avoid someone or something that is negatively impacting you, you can do a multitude of things.

First, it is critical to understand that it takes a strong internal foundation to avoid things that are bad for us. From consuming too much candy in one sitting to arguing with your parents about your curfew, whatever is coming against you may knock you off balance if you don't have a strong core that tells you right from wrong.

When it comes to eating too much candy, we know that high sugar intake isn't good for our bodies. If we consume too much sugar, this could cause us to gain weight, increase our chances of developing diabetes, and cause tooth decay. These types of defenses against us can negatively affect our bodies, possibly causing future health issues that may be incurable. However, if you have a strong foundation and remember what you have been taught about sugar consumption, you have the choice to pivot away from making a bad decision.

In the same way, if we continue to fight with our parents over things we know have been put in place for our best interests, then what is against you may win. Your parents have a set of rules for a reason. Hopefully these rules are in place to mold you into a constructive adult one day. Even if the rules seem unbearable to you, they are set for a reason and they are beyond your control. Understanding this concept can help you pivot from getting into situations with your parents that will ultimately negatively impact you. These negative impacts can include having restrictions placed on you and limited access to things you desire. The ideas regarding rules also relate to other areas, including school, your basketball team, and anything else that has some sort of organization to it. If the foundation has been set through rules, you can learn and follow them or go against them. The first choice leads to success, while the second leads to violations and failures.

Another way pivoting helps during a game is by allowing a player to find an opening on the basketball court to take a shot. This is critical if you want your team to ultimately win the game. Just like trying to move your body into a position to score, you can position your body to find a new direction in any given situation. If you have friends who are in a store and want to steal, you can pivot your body to go into a different direction and walk away from them. If you have a classmate who is trying to cheat off you during a test, you can literally pivot your body to block your answers from their view.

A strong pivot can make a play during a game or on the streets of life. As long as you understand that your foundation is key to making this move successful, this same idea will transfer over to your day-to-day decisions.

Pivot Failures

A five second violation can be called if a player holds onto the ball longer than five seconds once the established foot has been planted. This violation can cause the ball to be turned over to the defending team, possibly resulting in them scoring. This can lead you and your team to become frustrated and even fall behind in the game. In this same way, if you hold onto something too long, it can turn against you. If you hold on to information about someone without seeking help for them, the end result could be dire. Therefore, make sure your foundation is strong, but also be sure that you are following its guidelines.

Also, if you change your pivot foot or move your feet without dribbling, this could cause a violation. You have to make sure that you stand strong in your stance; weak stances will cause issues.

How will you overcome in life?

_____

_____

_____

_____

_____

_____

_____

_____

_____

Checking Emotions

It is very hard to keep your stance when you are pivoting. Whether it is the defenders against you, the shot clock, or a lack of open and available players to pass to, it can be very easy for a defender to knock you out of your stance. This can cause a number of different violations. Once you are comfortable with the foundation and requirements of a pivot, the more you practice, the stronger you will be in the stance.

In a similar sense, once you make a decision based off your foundation and values, you must stick to that decision. If you chose not to smoke cigarettes with your friends after school because you know it is bad for your body and you could get in a lot of trouble, then stick to your decision and just say no. Be strong in your decision and, just like when you pivot, don't let anything come against you and knock you off your strong foundation.

Sometimes a player can't choose their pivot foot. This situation can be frustrating, especially if you have a preference for a pivot foot or are becoming distracted by the aggressive defender in your face. Just like in life, there are times when we can't stop what happens to us. However, once we remember the foundation we have, we can make the right choice for our next steps. For instance, if you are in a situation that you did not choose to be in, like going to a party where others are now drinking, you can pivot yourself away from drinking. Even though others are looking like they are having the time of their lives while getting drunk, you don't have to let your current situation dictate your next move. Stay strong in your foundation and remember that pivoting in the wrong direction could lead to you altering not only your state of mind, but also the rest of your life.

Thinking about the defender who is against you can bring up strong feelings, especially if they are able either to steal the ball from you or cause a violation against you. Even though it may seem as if the defender has gotten over on you, your next moves can make or break the following plays.

In life, there will be times when things come against you. They may knock you out of bounds or into something even worse. If you have a solid foundation, you can analyze the situation at hand and find a way to escape or make a new move. However, succumbing to whatever is against you not only weakens your foundation, but causes you more errors and violations. For instance, if you allow your friends to influence you to do drugs, then these drugs will not only literally knock you off your feet, but could also cause serious and irreversible damage, potentially putting your life at risk. And for what? To impress your friends who may not have as strong of a foundation as you and are willing to lose their balance impress others? Trust me. It's never worth it.

How will you check your emotions?

_____

_____

_____

_____

_____

_____

_____

_____

_____

Crossover

The Fundamentals

To successfully crossover, you need to be able to dribble with each hand. Once you are used to dribbling using each hand, then you can practice switching the ball from one hand to the other. Crossing the ball in front of your body from side to side is a crossover. This crossing movement enables an easy change in direction, which is your goal.

A crossover is used to get your defender off-balance, and once you do it, a number of things can happen. You can penetrate past the defender and drive the basketball to the basket to score or kick it out to others. You can also make time for a teammate to get open so you can pass to them, allowing them a chance to score.

A great example of someone who was effective with their crossovers is NBA great Allen Iverson. One time, he even crossed Michael Jordan (MJ). MJ was a great defender, but Iverson was a great dribbler. He used quick dribbles while mixing them with crossover moves, and doing so was able to cross MJ and score.

How will you build a strong foundation?

_____
_____
_____
_____
_____
_____
_____
_____
_____
_____

The Purpose

The purpose of the crossover is to get the defender off-balance. This can create an opportunity to take a shot or make time for others to get open themselves. If you are dribbling down the court and the defender is in front of you, you can either cross from right to left or from left to right. For instance, if you are on the right side of the court, you can use a crossover to get the defender off-balance. This may open a path for you to move down the left side of the court.

In life, we have to make specific moves for a reason. Just like the intent of a crossover is to cause confusion, you have to make sure that the moves you make will yield the intended outcomes. Because there are so many different things that can come against you, it takes time, training, and discipline to be able to effectively sell a crossover.

As a basketball player, basketball itself can consume your life. If you allow it to, it can and will become 100% of your focus. Even though this is a great idea when you are on the court, this mindset may not help you out when you step off the court. You want to be more than just a great player because obstacles and opportunities are always around, and if you are only focused on one area, then you will miss others. This will eventually catch up to you and possibly have a negative impacting your future.

One thing that could be negatively impacted is your body. If you get hurt on or off the court, your basketball career could be in jeopardy. If so, what immediate action(s) would you be able to take if you could no longer play basketball? Have you taken the time to think about a back-up plan? If you haven't, that could be detrimental to your future, just like a bad crossover could be detrimental to you trying to score.

There has to be a plan in sight if the direction you have started to go down is being blocked. Having a backup plan is imperative for your future. Are you focused in school, along with being a great player? Are you taking as much time to prepare and study for classes as you are to prepare for your next game? Are you learning skills in other areas, like business, entrepreneurship, and life, so that you can be successful in everything you do?

There will be a time when your days on the basketball court are numbered. It might be due to age, injury, or life issues in general. When you are done with basketball, what will you do next? You need to have a plan that is actively being developed alongside your basketball skills. Players like Lebron and Jordan have been extremely successful on and off the court because they were able to crossover into multiple arenas. How are you striving to be able to do the same?

Do you know your purpose? What is it?

_____

_____

_____

_____

_____

_____

_____

_____

_____

Crossover Failures

A good crossover will get a defender off of you. The goal is for them to move in the opposite direction as where you are going. A crossover failure may be due to you not setting it up correctly. If you don't sell a crossover, then it won't work.

Just like in life, if you don't have the right setup for yourself, then you aren't able to fool anyone. If you don't study for a test and ultimately fail, you have not fooled your teacher. If you lied to your parents about something and they find out the truth later, then you have set yourself up for failure. Just as the crossover, when done right, is a thoughtful move by a basketball player, you should have intent and awareness behind the moves you make in the rest of your life.

How will you overcome in life?

_____

_____

_____

_____

_____

_____

_____

_____

_____

Checking Emotions

The crossover is an emotionless move. If you act based on your feelings, you can make a mistake. Remember that your practice of the crossover has set you up to be able to handle any defender in your way. Being able to keep your emotions in check on the court will only support your efforts.

In the real world, we also have to keep our emotions in check. Even though we can have things come against us, how we handle each situation will determine the outcome. Have you been training to keep your emotions in check? Here are a couple of things that you can consider to either get on the path of stable emotions or continue to build a stronger emotional foundation.

Have you taken the time to understand your emotions and how they can impact your daily life? When you get sad, do you stay sad long? When you are angry at one person, do you share that anger with everyone that comes along your path? You have to really take the time to understand why you feel the way you feel. It is okay to experience negative emotions but, just like the crossover, you should immediately switch gears to create an opportunity for healing, restoration, or forgiveness.

Are you able to be calm when things come against you? For example, if a friend confronts you about a rumor that they heard you started about them, do you return their same confrontational energy back to them, or do you recognize their emotions then choose to react with emotions that are supportive? It is important to be able to stand strong against adversity and be in the right mind to respond to it. If you go off your emotions, you can potentially increase the negative energy in the situation, and even lose a friend.

Do you hold onto what has gone wrong in your life? If so, how will you be able to make the next moves if you are thinking about past ones? Unfortunately, life goes on with or without us. If we are stuck in yesterday, then we won't be making any crossovers in the future. You have to let go of that missed shot you made a few minutes earlier to be able to make the next. You have to let go of the bad grade you may have gotten on a test so that you can prepare for the next one. Carrying the weight of what has been done only slows your efforts in what you are trying to do. Just like the crossover, make a quick move, change directions, and keep going.

How will you check your emotions?

_____

_____

_____

_____

_____

_____

_____

_____

Pump Fake

The Fundamentals

The foundation of a pump fake is a jump shot. However, when doing a jump shot, you actually jump off the floor. When doing a pump fake, you refrain from jumping. This is how you 'fake' out the defender. You are holding the ball in a shooting form as if you are about to leave the floor and jump, but you actually don't! This move is a fundamental move in basketball.

You have to use your head and eyes to try to sell the move as well as your body. It's very important to sell the shot as if you are truly about to make it, but ultimately you know that you aren't actually going to shoot the ball. A pump fake has to be believable for it to be successful.

How will you build a strong foundation?

_____

_____

_____

_____

_____

_____

_____

_____

_____

The Purpose

The purpose of a pump fake is to make the defender think you are going to shoot the basketball, but your true intentions are the opposite. By doing this, the defender may jump to block the attempted shot, giving you the opportunity to make another move.

Furthermore, the defender may become confused, giving you multiple options for what to do next. You may be able to drive the ball to the basket to score, or you may become free to take an actual shot since it allows you to get some room to make a move. Either way, a pump fake is a great way to try to confuse a defender who is in your face wanting to block your shot, take the ball, or cause a turnover. The more you try and sell it, the more often the defender will fall for it.

Sometimes in life, we have to cause confusion to be able to make the next move. We do this to not let everyone know our plans. It may seem like you are deceiving someone, but everyone doesn't need to know what you are doing. Trust me, the fewer who know the better. When we let everyone give us their opinions, we can end up living lives that aren't ours.

Pump Fake Failures

When trying to pump fake, there are a number of things that can go wrong. For instance, the defender can cause you to travel if your foundation isn't strong. If the defender knows that the pump fake is indeed a fake shot, this could cause him or her to get even closer to you.

Moreover, if you don't sell the shot well enough, the defender isn't going anywhere. He or she may stay in their same position, potentially causing you to lose the ball or lose your balance. For these reasons it's very important to practice the pump fake. If you aren't confident doing it, it will show.

In life, we may be able to fool some people, but not everyone. Therefore, you have to practice keeping a straight face and keeping your agenda intact. You have to remember what you have set out to do and stick to it.

How will you overcome in life?

_____

_____

_____

_____

_____

_____

_____

_____

_____

Checking Emotions

There are many examples of how the concept of a pump fake can come in handy. A pump fake can also be described as doing one thing to cover up what you really want or need to do, which is something else.

A good example of a pump fake in life is if you have obligations to take care of for your parents, but your friends want you to go with them somewhere. In this case, you have to make a decision. The idea of the pump fake can be used here by telling your friend you may meet them later, but you decide to go and do what you need to do. In this way, saying one thing with the intentions of doing something else may come off as a lie. However, the reality is that you have obligations you need to fulfill. You might need to make whatever excuse you can to take care of business.

Another example has to do with telling everyone your business and dreams. Some things should be kept to yourself. If you stay behind the scenes instead of announcing every step to whoever will listen, then things will eventually work out. The element of surprise is a great thing.

How will you check your emotions?

_____

_____

_____

_____

_____

_____

_____

_____

_____

Passing

The Fundamentals

There are many ways to pass a ball. A chest pass is when you pass the ball straight from your chest to the chest of one of your teammates. A bounce pass is when you bounce the ball down across the court floor to get it to your teammate. Regardless of what kind of pass you use, you want to make sure it is strong enough to get to the player it is intended to go to.

But before you pass the ball, you need to make sure to look around the court to see who is available. This is imperative and will help prevent you from passing the ball to the defending team, which could result in unnecessary points being scored against your team.

How will you build a strong foundation?

_____

_____

_____

_____

_____

_____

_____

_____

_____

The Purpose

One of the many purposes of passing the ball is to move it around the court. Any player can pass the ball, but it takes a strong level of teamwork to be successful. Therefore, passing is not a selfish act. The team's mission is to drive the action of the game by passing the ball as a collective group. However, you have to know what you are going to do before passing the ball. Will it be a chest pass or a bounce pass? In which direction will you pass the ball? Do you remember why you are even passing the ball in the first place?

Another reason to pass the ball is to create an opportunity for a shot, which is the ultimate goal. Passing the ball amongst teammates allows the players to strategically move around to create opportunities for one person to take the lead and shoot the ball. Finding an open person can be hard when the defense is being aggressive, but this is the only way to create opportunities to get some points.

Even though there are many reasons to pass a ball, the pass itself depends on the play being executed. Your teammates should already know where each player is or will be because you all have practiced this before. The practices, called pass drills, are set up to strengthen the ability of the team to move the ball into a position to be able to score. By doing pass drills, teammates are able to get into a groove through repetition. These drills can be done 15 minutes at a time, but the time spent practicing is beyond valuable. It helps to build collaboration amongst the teammates, and also allows the team to become stronger as a unit. People need a strong unit around them to be successful and basketball is not an exception to that rule.

When it comes to life, we should always have a purpose for the passes we make. Just like in basketball, we have to know where we can pass, how to pass, and what our purpose is. If you want to be a successful basketball player, then you know that your effort in a game is not the only thing that leads to a win. It is the combined effort of all the players on the team, including the effort and teamwork put into successfully passing the ball. Think, what are you passing to others? Hopefully, whatever you are passing is positive. Perhaps it's a kind act, like holding the door open for someone. Maybe you are passing high fives, handshakes, or hugs. You could be passing judgement, threats, or something negative. It all really depends on you and the choices you make.

Practicing how to pass positive things to others can be beneficial, especially if you come from an environment that is not conducive to exhibiting positive behaviors. It may be harder to pass on something that you aren't used to receiving, but it can still be done. This can be achieved by actively practicing how to be the positive person you want to be on and off the court. Just like a team does pass drills, you need to practice your own life drills.

You can practice being a positive person in a number of different ways. Try to recognize when others are passing something negative onto you and then do the opposite. However, it does take time to actively identify when someone has hurt you, and often we react before we think. However, taking the time to think before you react is something that you can practice. You can also ask for help from a counselor, teacher, or someone positive in your life who you know you can trust to help you practice passing on positive things to others recognizing when something positive is being passed onto you. Another option is to try to be of service to others and find opportunities to pass something nice or positive on to someone else. You could volunteer at your school, church, mosque, temple, local garden, library, or anywhere else that could use your time. Finding ways to put others first is not only selfless, it shows that you can be an all-around top athlete who can successfully pass on and off the court.

Do you know your purpose? What is it?

_____

_____

_____

_____

_____

_____

_____

_____

Pass Failures

A bad pass can happen at any moment. If the pass isn't strong enough, it probably won't get to the player that you are passing it to. If the pass is too strong, then it can either hurt the player you are passing it to or shoot past them. Also, if you aren't paying attention, a pass can be on its way to you and you may miss it, get hit by it, or end up losing control of the ball. If that happens, the defender may get a hold of the ball and steal it from you before you get a chance to recover.

Think about your life now. What type of things are you passing onto others? Are you passing on positive vibes? Are you in positions to be of service? Are you lending a hand when others are in need? Do you have an attitude or demeanor that understands that life consists of more than you and your needs? Do you realize that there are things that you can pass on that can positively impact others? All these questions are here to get you thinking about your actions and the roles you play in others' lives.

In the same way, do you realize that there are things that you can pass on that hurt others? Think about it. Have you ever been rude to someone because they were rude to you? Have you ever hurt someone that hurt you? Have you ever thought negative thoughts about a player or teammate because they did something that wasn't nice or supportive? If we only passed on the negative things that others have passed on to us, then what type of world would we live in? Would this world be safe, secure, and positive? Would it be a world where you want your parents, siblings, grandparents or future children living? I think not.

It is imperative that you think about what you are passing on and how you are doing it. Just like in basketball, there is a purpose for passing. What is your purpose for the things that you pass on? When you do want to pass on something negative, you should really evaluate the reasons why and attempt to things out before continuing a negative cycle that does not support growth, achievement, success, or happiness.

How will you overcome in life?

_____

_____

_____

_____

_____

_____

_____

_____

_____

Checking Emotions

During a game of basketball, the other team's entire mission, when on defense, is to steal the ball from your team so that they can score. You can't always stop their mission or even change it, but you are always in control of how you respond.

Another barrier is time. The game of basketball is a timed event with a clock that keeps on counting down. If you have limited time to pass something, then you may do it recklessly, in a hurry and without proper preparations. Just like in life, we are fighting against a clock. We have set times to turn in our homework, come inside for the night, and attend class, to name a few. Having an understanding of this will make for a stronger foundation from within and allow the pass or exchange to be more fluid and structured, instead of quick and abrupt.

Now, there are times when someone passes something to us and the outcomes are out of our control. Therefore, it is strongly urged that you recognize what type of energy you have before, during, and after the pass or exchange. How do you feel when you see someone coming your way that you have had bad interactions with? Are you already on high alert and ready to battle before there is even an exchange of words or movements? Do the hairs on the back of your neck stand up being in the presence of this person? If they do, that's okay. At least you are recognizing your emotions before anything has even occurred. This is the right time to check your emotions, get them in order, and be ready to receive whatever is thrown your way. It is important that you are prepared, because when it comes to emotions, we can quickly pass positive or negative energy to others before we even realize it.

Therefore, preparing to pass positive energy to others is essential. This can be done by passing on compliments, having positive conversations, and exuding good energy. Even if you sometimes feel that the world is against you, you don't have to be against the world. You can be the change that the world needs, on and off the court. Conversely, you can also be negative and end up limiting opportunities for yourself. Furthermore, you may pass the wrong thing to the wrong person, and that person could end up being the decision maker for something you really want or need. You could be risking everything because you decided to pass something negative onto someone else, not realizing how detrimental this negative pass could be to someone who isn't as emotionally stable as you.

How will you check your emotions?

_____

_____

_____

_____

_____

_____

_____

_____

Defense

The Fundamentals

When you are on defense, you have to do a number of things. You have to keep your arms up or out to try and prevent the offensive player from being able to pass the ball or score. If your arms are up and in the way, they may not be able to pass the ball. This opens the possibility of you getting possession of the ball.

When the offensive player stops and dribbles the ball, you can have your arms spread out. With them out, you can wave them to block the offensive player from being able to pass. If the offensive player in front of you doesn't have the ball, then you can block him or her from being able to receive it.

Regardless, of the position of your arms, you need to have your knees bent. However, this does change depending on what position the defensive player is in. If the player can't dribble the ball anymore, then you can stand straight up so they can't get a good look around the court. You want to match the offensive player, always making sure that you are creating some sort of barrier for them.

Furthermore, you want to be sure you are watching the ball. This will help you to find opportunities to steal the ball away from the offensive player. It can also make it more difficult for the player to shoot if you are focused on the ball and where it is. By watching the ball, you can better block or stop them from passing the ball to others.

How will you build a strong foundation?

_____

_____

_____

_____

_____

_____

_____

_____

_____

The Purpose

While on defense, your goal is to stop offensive players from being able to move, pass, or shoot the ball. You have to do everything possible to stop them. In life, there are times when we need to be on the defense with others. Maybe you have a friend who has come to you with a bad idea that you know will not yield rewarding or positive results. You may have to be on defense and convince them that their idea is not a good one. You may have to attempt to block them from going down a path that isn't right for them. You may have to do whatever it takes to stop them.

On the other hand, you may have things that come up against you and attempt to block you from making your next move. You might have to find a way to get around them, but sometimes whatever is coming up against you may be needed. For example, if you are driving and you come up to a sign that reads *DETOUR*, then that sign is there for a reason. There may be possible construction ahead, or even an accident. Regardless of the reason, the sign is serving as a defense to block you from going a way that might be wrong or even dangerous. This type of defense isn't bad, it is actually extremely helpful. Ultimately, you have to be able to identify if the defense against you is helpful or harmful.

Do you know your purpose? What is it?

_____

_____

_____

_____

_____

_____

_____

_____

_____

Defense Failures

When you're on defense, things can go wrong. For instance, if you have a bad stance, the offensive player may be able to drive right past you. They may also be able to get a good look at the court to try to make a different move, or they might go through your arms if they aren't controlled.

In life, if we don't have a strong defense against bad things, we may become a victim of the negative situations around us. If someone comes to you and asks you to take some drugs and you have a weak defense, then you might do it. If you don't have a strong stance against eating unhealthy food, then you may not have enough confidence to stand against it. Similarly, imagine you have a friend who wants to fight another friend. Perhaps you have the ability to influence your friend and persuade them to avoid starting the fight. If you don't have a strong foundation in your argument for avoiding the fight, then your defensive move may not be successful.

How will you overcome in life?

_____

_____

_____

_____

_____

_____

_____

Checking Emotions

Life can be hard sometimes. There are many things that can block you from success, just like in basketball. In life, when something comes against us, we have to check our emotions and make sure that we stay in control. Keep your joy and keep a smile on your face. Many times, these types of acts frustrate whatever is against you, and that's ok. Misery loves company, but you don't want to keep this type of company. You should stay on your toes and be ready to make the next move around the defenses against you.

Life is a challenge. Every day brings new battles. Sometimes we are prepared for them, sometimes we are not. It's important to protect yourself from the outside world that is trying to attack you. You can't let your emotions take you on a path that isn't good for you or that may lead to severe consequences. You need to remember to have a strong stance and morals. If everyone is cheating on a test, you don't have to do it. You can keep your integrity and take the test honestly. If everyone is cussing, you don't have to entertain it. Ultimately, you have to protect your heart and soul, and sometimes you can help others do the same for themselves. Just imagine yourself as a soldier in battle. A soldier is always prepared. If something comes against them, they are prepared to attack or avoid it in whatever way they need to.

How will you check your emotions?

_____

_____

_____

_____

_____

_____

_____

_____

_____

Rebound

The Fundamentals

A rebound happens when the ball hits the rim or backboard instead of going into the basket, and comes back down onto the court. Every player who is near the rim will be attempting to get the rebound. Players use their legs to jump as high as they can to get the rebound. Sometimes there are several players trying to get the rebound, or only one player from each team is there. Regardless of how many players are around, each wants to be the first to touch the ball in order to gain control of it for their team.

If you are the lucky player who gets control of the ball, you then have to be strong and hold the ball as tightly as you can. The rebounder should squeeze the ball and have it centered to their chest with their elbows out. This will keep other players from trying to poke the rebounder or steal the ball. You may hear your coach telling you to put your elbows out when you're rebounding. This is because most of your strength is in the center in this position.

How will you build a strong foundation?

_____

_____

_____

_____

_____

_____

_____

_____

_____

The Purpose

The purpose of getting a rebound for either team is to gain control of the ball. If a team misses a shot, then they want to get the rebound to attempt to make another shot, and the defending team wants the rebound so that they can attempt a shot. Furthermore, rebounds only happen at the basket. There is a time and place for this action to occur. When we think about life, there is also a time and place for things to happen. There is a time to study and a time to hang out with friends. There is a time to clean and a time to get messy. There is even a time to have fun and a time to be serious. There is a time for everything, so make sure that you are doing what you should be at any given time.

Moreover, in the same way that a rebound has a purpose, your actions off the court should have a purpose too. Are you taking the time to prepare yourself for the next day the night before? Are you attending classes consistently to gain more knowledge so that you can be a good student as well as a great basketball player? Or are you preparing yourself for failure by not turning in assignments, taking tests, or completing projects? Are you always late to work, causing unnecessary issues at your job? We all know that our actions speak louder than words. In basketball, your actions should serve the purpose of the game. Your actions outside of basketball prepare you for success or failure as well. It is up to you to decide that you will be in control of yourself and your situation.

Rebound Failures

If you don't have a tight grip on the ball when you get the rebound, then another player can knock the ball out of your hand as you are coming down with it. If you bring the ball too low, it can get knocked out of your hands as well. If you aren't paying attention to your surroundings, you can lose control of the ball due to a defender who is more focused. Regardless of the cause, when you lose control of the ball you give the opposing team a chance to gain control and score.

In life, things get knocked out of our control all the time. This might happen more than we want it to, so we need to make sure that our moves are calculated in a way that supports our efforts %100. We should always have situational awareness, which means that we are aware of our surroundings, and we should follow through on our actions. In the same way that you have to follow through with a rebound and make sure you do whatever it takes to get the ball, you have to do whatever it takes to complete the tasks at hand.

How will you overcome in life?

_____

_____

_____

_____

_____

_____

_____

_____

Checking Emotions

During a rebound, there can be a number of different players from each team going for the ball at the same time. This can cause tension and aggression, and also cause a player to second guess themselves and not complete the rebound successfully. During an active rebound, one of the players can end up crashing down to the ground without the ball. If this happens, does the basketball player stay down and become angry with everyone around them? Of course not! The player gets back up and keeps playing in the game.

Think about a time when something came against you and set you back. How did you react? Did you let the situation get to you or motivate you to stop? I surely hope not! Regardless of what happens to us, it's important that we bounce back. If you take a test and don't get the grade you wanted, then you can either stay depressed about it, or you can bounce back and determine to do better next time. You can study harder, think of different strategies to pass the next test, or even just review what you did the first time so that you don't make the same mistakes again.

Regardless of the setback, you have to keep pushing forward. A player doesn't stop the game if they miss a shot. They just bounce back and continue to play. Just like you're determined to be the best basketball player you can be, you should also be thinking about being the best person you can be. The only way to do that is to bounce back when things come against you. Never give up, because there will always be an opportunity for a rebound, an opportunity to try again, so be sure to look for ways to keep moving forward.

How will you check your emotions?

_____
_____
_____
_____
_____
_____
_____
_____
_____

Conclusion

Congratulations to you for taking the time to not only develop your basketball skills by learning more about the fundamentals of this great game, but by taking the time to identify ways to improve your life off the court, such as at home, in the classroom, and out in public. Life is a journey filled with many highs and lows. We will experience ups and downs along the way. Regardless of what we experience, it's how we deal with these experiences that determines whether we will be successful in life.

Always remember that the game is not over until the last buzzer, and life isn't over until the last breath has been taken. Never give up on your dreams and desires, and do whatever need to get to the next level, regardless of what the next level is. It's not over until you have no breath left in your lungs. Always Think First and keep pushing forward with everything you have. You only have one life, so live it to its fullest!

About the Author

Travis Garrison grew up in Suitland, Maryland with his mother and two older brothers. He was a star at DeMatha Catholic High School where he played for the legendary Hall of Fame coach Morgan Wootten. His individual honors include being a McDonald's All-American, a Michael Jordan All-Star, and a Washington Post All-Met player. He graduated from DeMatha in June 2002. Coach Gary Williams recruited Travis to play for his defending National Champion Maryland Terrapins. He was part of a highly touted recruiting class that led Maryland to its first ACC title in twenty years. Travis was a three-year starter and his up and down career at Maryland are an important part of why he wrote his book, Never Satisfied: An Athlete's Battle. After some post-draft workouts for NBA teams and the NBA D-League, Travis was Rookie of the Year in the CBA playing for the Great Falls Explorers in Montana. In addition to playing in North America, his basketball skills have taken him to teams in South America, Asia, Europe, and Eastern Europe. Off the court, Travis is passionate about helping others, especially young players.

Additional Title by Travis Garrison

Available at www.think-first.net

CPSIA information can be obtained
at www.ICGtesting.com
Printed in the USA
FSHW010700090222

9 781734 811308